T0413891

THE WORLD OF OCEAN ANIMALS

POLAR BEARS

by Mari Schuh

Ideas for Parents and Teachers

Pogo Books let children practice reading informational text while introducing them to nonfiction features such as headings, labels, sidebars, maps, and diagrams, as well as a table of contents, glossary, and index.

Carefully leveled text with a strong photo match offers early fluent readers the support they need to succeed.

Before Reading

- "Walk" through the book and point out the various nonfiction features. Ask the student what purpose each feature serves.
- Look at the glossary together. Read and discuss the words.

Read the Book

- Have the child read the book independently.
- Invite him or her to list questions that arise from reading.

After Reading

- Discuss the child's questions. Talk about how he or she might find answers to those questions.
- Prompt the child to think more. Ask: What did you know about polar bears before reading this book? What more would you like to learn?

Pogo Books are published by Jump!
5357 Penn Avenue South
Minneapolis, MN 55419
www.jumplibrary.com

Library of Congress Cataloging-in-Publication Data

Names: Schuh, Mari C., 1975- author.
Title: Polar bears / Mari Schuh.
Description: Minneapolis, MN: Jump!, Inc., [2022]
Series: The world of ocean animals
Includes index. | Audience: Ages 7-10
Identifiers: LCCN 2020057960 (print)
LCCN 2020057961 (ebook)
ISBN 9781636900667 (hardcover)
ISBN 9781636900674 (paperback)
ISBN 9781636900681 (ebook)
Subjects: LCSH: Polar bear—Juvenile literature.
Classification: LCC QL737.C27 S3538 2022 (print)
LCC QL737.C27 (ebook) | DDC 599.786—dc23
LC record available at https://lccn.loc.gov/2020057960
LC ebook record available at https://lccn.loc.gov/2020057961

Editor: Jenna Gleisner
Designer: Michelle Sonnek

Photo Credits: iStock, cover; Sergey Smolin/Shutterstock, 1; Eric Isselee/Shutterstock, 3; FloridaStock/Shutterstock, 4, 6-7, 12-13; Francois Gohier/Pantheon/SuperStock, 5; imageBROKER/Alamy, 8-9; Trevor Tennant/Shutterstock, 10-11; Alexey Seafarer/Shutterstock, 14, 20-21; Samantha Crimmin/Alamy, 15; Gerald Corsi/iStock, 16-17; Matthias Breiter/Minden Pictures/SuperStock, 18; robertharding/Alamy, 19; ILYA AKINSHIN/Shutterstock, 23.

Printed in the United States of America at Corporate Graphics in North Mankato, Minnesota.

TABLE OF CONTENTS

CHAPTER 1

BIG BEARS

A polar bear walks slowly on the ice. Turning its head from side to side, the hungry bear begins its hunt.

Polar bears are the biggest bears in the world. Males can weigh up to 1,700 pounds (771 kilograms). They are nearly 10 feet (3.0 meters) tall when they stand on their hind legs!

Polar bears live in the Arctic. It is very cold and icy. They spend a lot of time on floating ice. They also swim in water near the **coast**.

TAKE A LOOK!

Where do polar bears live? Take a look!

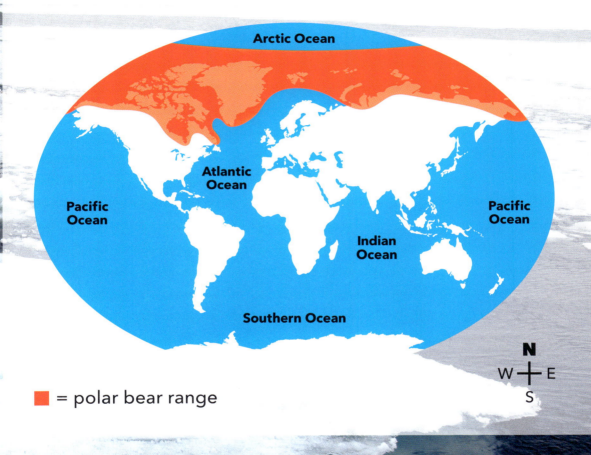

Arctic Ocean

Atlantic Ocean

Pacific Ocean

Pacific Ocean

Indian Ocean

Southern Ocean

N
W E
S

■ = polar bear range

Polar bears are built for life in the Arctic. Large, wide paws act like **snowshoes**. They help the bears walk on snow and ice. Each paw can be as wide as a dinner plate!

The ice is slippery. Bumpy pads on their furry paws keep them from slipping. Sharp claws help, too.

TAKE A LOOK!

What are a polar bear's body parts called? Take a look!

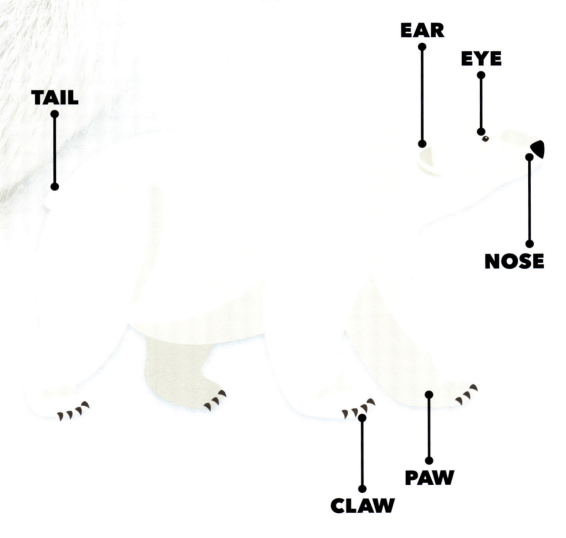

EAR

EYE

TAIL

NOSE

CLAW

PAW

A polar bear's fur looks white. But it is actually clear! The hairs are **hollow**. They **reflect** sunlight, making them look white. The light color acts as **camouflage**. The fur blends in with snow and ice.

Underneath, polar bears have black skin. The dark color helps them **absorb** heat from the sun.

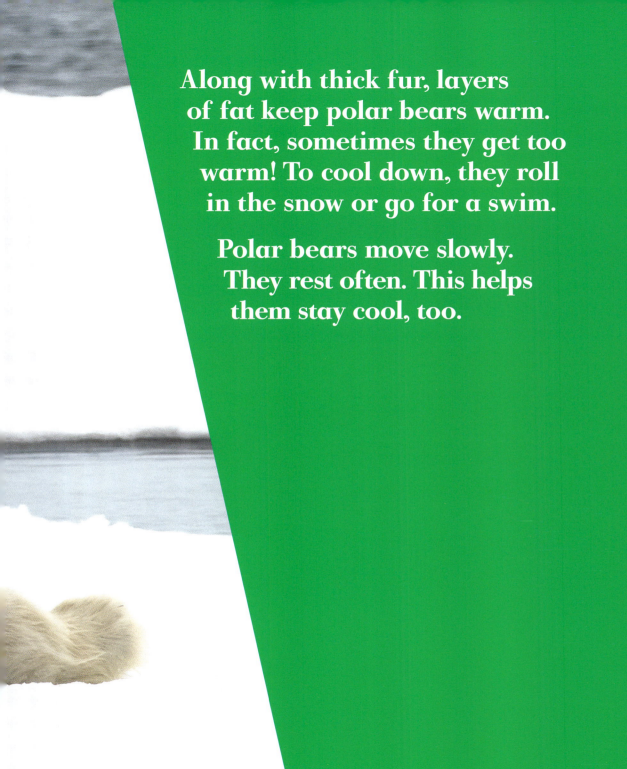

Along with thick fur, layers of fat keep polar bears warm. In fact, sometimes they get too warm! To cool down, they roll in the snow or go for a swim.

Polar bears move slowly. They rest often. This helps them stay cool, too.

CHAPTER 2

ON THE HUNT

Polar bears are at the top of their **food chain**. No animals hunt them. This makes them **apex predators**. Polar bears mainly hunt seals. But they eat dead whales, narwhals, and walruses, too. They also eat eggs, berries, and **kelp**.

Polar bears are smart hunters. They use their powerful sense of smell to find seals' breathing holes in the ice. Then they wait. They might wait for hours or days. When seals come up for air, polar bears use their sharp claws to grab them.

seal hole

Polar bears need ice to hunt seals. But **climate change** is melting ice earlier each season. This gives polar bears less time to hunt. Less ice also means polar bears have to swim farther to find ice.

DID YOU KNOW?

Polar bears use only their front legs to swim. This way of swimming is unusual. But it works well for polar bears. They are strong swimmers. They can swim for many hours at a time!

CHAPTER 3

POLAR BEAR CUBS

In the fall, a female gets ready to give birth. She builds a **den** in a **snowdrift** or in the ground.

den •••••▶

Like most **mammals**, female polar bears give birth to live young. Tiny **cubs** are born in the winter. They drink their mothers' milk. Dens keep them safe and warm as they grow.

In the spring, cubs are ready to leave their dens. Mothers teach their cubs how to hunt and swim. They keep their cubs safe. Cubs learn how to live in the cold Arctic.

DID YOU KNOW?

Females usually have two cubs at a time.

ACTIVITIES & TOOLS

GUESS THE SMELL

Polar bears use their sense of smell to find seals. Test your sense of smell with this fun guessing game!

What You Need:
- five food items with strong odors (such as lemons, onions, broccoli, cinnamon, coffee, cheese, bananas, garlic, or hardboiled eggs)
- five small plastic containers with lids
- one friend or family member
- bandana or large cloth napkin to use as a blindfold

1. Put each food item in a separate plastic container. Seal the lids. Don't let your friend see the food.

2. Have your friend sit down and put on a blindfold.

3. Ask your friend to sniff the foods in the containers one at a time. Can your friend guess the foods only by their scents? Are some foods easier to identify than others?

4. Make a chart that shows which foods your friend correctly identified.

5. Have your friend choose other food items for you to smell. Your turn!

GLOSSARY

absorb: To take in.

apex predators: Predators at the top of a food chain that are not hunted by any other animal.

camouflage: A disguise or natural coloring that allows animals to hide by making them look like their surroundings.

climate change: Changes in Earth's weather and climate over time.

coast: The land next to an ocean or sea.

cubs: Young polar bears.

den: The home of a wild animal.

food chain: An ordered arrangement of animals and plants in which each feeds on the one below it in the chain.

hollow: Empty inside.

kelp: Large brown seaweed that grows in the ocean.

mammals: Warm-blooded animals that give birth to live young, which drink milk from their mothers.

reflect: To throw back light from a surface.

snowdrift: A pile of snow created by wind.

snowshoes: Webbed frames shaped like rackets that attach to boots to keep feet from sinking in snow.

INDEX

TO LEARN MORE

Finding more information is as easy as 1, 2, 3.

1 Go to www.factsurfer.com

2 Enter "polarbears" into the search box.

3 Choose your book to see a list of websites.

FACT SURFER